MONSTER MAX'S SHARK SPAGHETTI

Claire Freedman

Illustrated by **Sue Hendra**
and **Paul Linnet**

BLOOMSBURY

LONDON NEW DELHI NEW YORK SYDNEY

Today Max and his monster friends

for lots of stinky summer fun —
they just can't wait. Hooray!

Max hopes the hotel food tastes yum
but, just in case, he packs
a stash of stale dung beetle crisps —
his favourite smelly snacks!

All monsters fly with Queasy Jet.
Max loves their in-flight meal —

moth mash with tapeworm sausages,
washed down with puréed eel.

Their hotel is delightful,
sticky slug trails paint the walls.
The ceiling's draped with spiders —
wheee! Look out for when one falls!

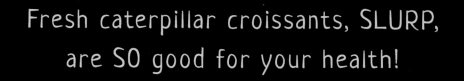

Fresh caterpillar croissants, SLURP,
are SO good for your health!

CRASH! BANG! comes from the kitchen.
It's the gunkiest you've seen.

The dirty plates are being washed.
One monster licks them clean!

Yippee! It's time to hit the beach.
"It's scorching hot!" Max smiles.

His sunscreen whiffs of rotten eggs,
bugs come from miles and miles!

The beachfront has some super rides.
Max loves the GLOOP-THE-LOOP!
They whizz down chutes of slobber,
splashing through great vats of gloop!

GLOOP-THE-LOOP

The hotel's pond slime pool is great!
Staff bring scum shakes to sip,
with woodworm riddled loungers,
to relax after your dip!

It's their last meal at the hotel
and the friends get a HUGE fright.
Chef's cooked up SHARK SPAGHETTI –
it's the dish with extra BITE!

Max bravely digs his fork in but,
"STOP!" gasp his friends, "take care!"

Max prangs a slimy shark's tooth – PING!
It hits him – YEOWCH! Guess where?

Max has to stand the whole flight home.
His trip won't be forgotten.
He has a special souvenir —
the tooth pulled from his bottom!